PRISON BREAK

a Mary MacIntosh novel

MAUREEN ANNE MEEHAN

PRISON BREAK

www. maureenmeehanbooks.com

info@maureenmeehan.com

PRISON BREAK DEDICATION

To those who bear the weight of wrongful accusation, who fight unseen battles within walls not of their making – may justice one day find you, and may hope to be your constant companion.

And to the guards who walk the line, who see beyond the bars and into the hearts of those they protect and confine – may your duty always be tempered with compassion.

This book is for you.

PRISON BREAK AUTHOR'S NOTE
The Cracks in My Cage

I am the stone, the shadowy, forgotten beneath the sky. Bars are my horizon, but freedom sings nearby.

The walls close like whispers, secrets buried in the night. I claw for breath of morning, chained but burning with light.

These hands, they once built bridges, now they scrape for a way through. Each night, I map the cracks, dreaming of skies I never knew.

The stars can't see me here, nor the sun that hides its face. But in the dark, I'm shifting, unseen, I trace my place.

I'll become the wind one day, slip through the world unseen. And no lock will hold me back, from the man I've never been.

Table of Contents

Chapter 1

In the old days of baseball, there existed a tradition that when the manager of the team felt like they had secured a victory, he put a bag at the end of the team bench, confident that the lead would be a victory. Hence, the colloquialism of we "have it in the bag," meaning confidence in success. This phrase is universally used today to describe success or victory.

On July 19, 1910, Cy Young, one of baseball's greatest pitchers, played his 500th career game. At the time, he was pitching for the Cleveland Naps (now the Cleveland Guardians) in the American League. Young's career spanned from 1890 to 1911, and during that game, he set records that still stand today, including the most career wine (511). By 1910, he was already a legend, and reaching his 500th game further cemented his place in baseball history. His longevity and durability were remarkable, which is why the award for the best pitcher in Major League Baseball is named the "Cy Young Award" in his honor.

In 1910 at the Wyoming State Penitentiary in Rawlins, Wyoming, inmates were given the chance to delay or avoid their executions if they won baseball games against other prisoners or teams. If they lost, their execution would be carried out shortly thereafter. Tensions between local ranchers, gamblers, and the early oil barons ran high, leading to the mysterious death of a star player during the game. As Mary MacIntosh will discover as she delves sinto this cold case, clues might suggest that the game was more than just a sporting event. It was perhaps connected to a secret code passed along generations.

In 1903, a famous frontier scout, lawman, and hired gunman, Tom Horn was convicted of murder and hanged at the Wyoming State Penitentiary. Though Horn's execution was several years before 1910, his case remains one of the most famous in Wyoming's history.

Horn was known for his work as a Pinkerton detective and his involvement in conflicts between cattle ranchers and rustlers in the late 19th and early 20th centuries. He became infamous for his role as a range detective, hired to eliminate cattle thieves, but his methods were ruthless.

Horn was convicted of murder in 1903 for the shooting of 14-year-old Willie Nickel. The boy was mistakenly believed to be involved in cattle rustling, though there was significant debate about whether Horn was actually guilty of if he was set up as a scapegoat. Horn's trial was controversial, and many believe it was influenced by circumstantial evidence and Horn's own loose tongue.

He was hanged at the Wyoming State Penitentiary on November 20, 1903, maintaining his innocence until the end. His story has become part of Western folklore, often seen as a tragic figure of the American frontier, caught between law and outlaw.

Big Nose George Parrott was a notorious outlaw and train robber. He attempted to escape from the Wyoming State Penitentiary, was lynched by a mob in 1881, and his body was infamously used in medical experiments, including the making of a pair of shoes from his skin.

The Tipton Gang was another outlaw group active in Wyoming and other parts of the West during the late 1800s and early 1900s. Some of its members were incarcerated in Wyoming's state prison during the 1910 era for crimes like cattle rustling, robbery, and murder. It is said to be that members of the Tipton Gang participated in the "life or death baseball game" at the Wyoming State Penitentiary in 1910. It is said that some members of the Tipton Gang were also members of the Freemasons.

Chapter 2

In medieval bird hunting days, men would a "beater" which is a person who drives game out of areas of cover by swinging sticks or flags. Hence, to flush something out of get to the bottom of something came the term, "don't beat around the bush."

Freemasonry has a long history, and several notable or infamous figures have been associated with it. For example, Aleister Crowley (1875-1947) was known as a controversial occultist and mystic. He was involved in various esoteric organizations, including Freemasonry. He was also a founder of Thelema, a religious movement that promoted individualism and self-expression, but his darker persona earned him the title of "The Wickedest Man in the World."

Albert Pike (1809-1891) was a prominent figure in Freemasonry in the United States, especially known for his writings on Scottish Rite Freemasonry. Although highly respected within the Masonic circles, he was criticized for his alleged associations with the Confederacy and some of his views on race, particularly in his time as a Confederate general during the American Civil War.

Giuseppe Mazzini (1805-1872) was an Italian revolutionary and Freemason, he played a significant role in Italy's unification and was a leader in various secret societies. He has sometimes been accuse of conspiring in the creation of Masonic-based world order, and his name appears in various conspiracy theories, particularly in relation to the Illuminati.

Licio Gelli (1919-2015) was an Italian financier and head of the shadowy Masonic Lodge Propaganda Due (P2). The P2 lodge became infamous in the 1970s and 1980s due to its involvement in political and financial scandals in Italy, including the collapse of the Banco Ambrosiano and suspected links to the Mafia and political corruption.

Cagliostro (Giuseppe Balsamo) (1743-1795) was a flamboyant occultist and conman, who claimed to be an alchemist and healer, traveling across Europe and gaining fame and infamy. He was eventually arrested by the Roman Catholic Church and sentenced to life imprisonment. His association with Freemasonry, particular his founding of a Masonic branch known as the Egyptian Rite, made him an enigmatic figure.

Jack the Ripper, though never proven, was suggested to be a Freemason. He is better known as the 19th-century serial killer in London.

Chapter 3

Mary MacIntosh is a tall, lanky auburn-haired, brown-eyed prosecutor in Sheridan, Wyoming. She was recently married to the town Sheriff, Burg, and she is now four months pregnant with whom they just learned is a baby boy. When Burgess was with her in the exam room for the ultrasound, he cried openly with the good news. Burg has two adult daughters, and he was never blessed with the privilege of also raising a son. He was a guy's guy and loved to fish and camp and hike and play sports. He was in his late 40's and knew that he was going to be older than most dads at the preschool pick up line, but he was thrilled beyond words.

Mac was first time married and now first time pregnant and while outgrowing her business suits, she was delighted. She never dreamed of having a baby. She had a tumultuous childhood and if it wasn't for her boss, Harry, back in the days of first-out-of-law school training, she would have never had a father figure.

She and Burg were leaving the doctor's office when Burg got a call from dispatch. There had been an unreported plane crash in the Big Horn mountains surrounding Sherian and the rumors surrounding the crash eerily echoed the survival tale of the 1972 Air Force flight in the Andes. Among the wreckage of the Air Force flight, there was evidence of foul play and the survivors of the crash were hiding something. It was a cold case, but what Burg was describing to her would require an investigation by his team and hers.

Chapter 4

Burg had just dropped Mac off at the Sheridan County Courthouse where her office was located when he got another call about a ruthless killer who had just escaped the Wyoming State Penitentiary in Rawlins, Wyoming. The report was that he headed north toward the Sheridan vicinity and during his time at the State Pen, he spoke often of being a descendant to one of the surviving witnesses to the 1910 "life or death baseball game" at the Wyoming State Penitentiary. He bragged often of the secret code that the prisoners used to gain favor with guards and only prisoners who were also members of the Freemasons knew the secret code.

This plane crash and the prison escape discovery on the same early Spring day was big news in Wyoming. It would turn out to be far more sinister than expected, linked by shadowy conspiracy involving a secret society than spanned generations.

Chapter 5

It was folklore in Wyoming back in the day that the 1910 baseball game was actually a front for a meeting between high-ranking Masons, who were using it to pass along a crucial piece of information – a code hidden within the design of the dollar bill. The game ended tragically when one of the Masons was murdered, and the code allegedly disappeared.

But Mac was discovering with her research on the plane crash in the Big Horn Mountains that survivors of the 1972 Air Force plane crash also possessed this knowledge, passed down through generations.

She felt like she was going down a rabbit hole, and perhaps she was, but escaped convict from 1977 Ted Bundy was apparently a modern Masonic. He used his knowledge of secret rituals and symbols – many of which are tied to the dollar bill – to manipulate people and stay ahead of law enforcement. It is rumored that his prison break was orchestrated by a shadowy faction within the Masons, who wanted him to retrieve something left behind at the site of the 1910 baseball game: an artifact linked to the design of the Great Seal on the dollar bill.

The seemingly mundane 1910 baseball game was actually a diversion for the Masons, who were hiding something of great value in Wyoming – a treasure linked to the hidden symbols on the dollar bill. Rumors of this treasure were passed through within the prison system, and recently, a secret group on board the ill-fated flight was trying to locate it when the plane crashed.

A document known as the "Unfinished Pyramid" was central to the Masonic rituals, and its design influenced the layout of the symbols on the dollar bill. The murder at the 1910 baseball game was over possession of this document, and now, one of the passengers who was a descendent of the plane crash might be in possession of it, likely unknowingly, holding the key to a dangerous secret.

Rumer had it that this document revealed plans for a new world order, orchestrated by rogue faction of the Masons. The escapee from 1977, Ted Bundy, was part of this faction, and this group will stop at nothing to retrieve the blueprint and carry out their plans.

Chapter 6

"You are not going to believe this," Mac pronounced as she walked through the door with Chinese takeout and a stack of files. Burg jumped to her rescue and grabbed the two sacks of food. He knew better than to touch her work files.

He unpacked the dinner for two (or three at this point) and listened to her explain.

"I am researching this plane crash and this prison break and my paralegal, who is smarter than me, put together this strange web of conspiracy that I am not sure what to do with it," Mac explained.

Burg continued to unpack the sweet and sour chicken that he preferred the aromatic shrimp that she liked and the sauteed green Seshwan beans that they both enjoyed while listening to her explain.

"So, this life and death prison baseball game in the Wyoming State Pen in 1910 was a ruse for a Masonic meeting of the Freemasons, but it went dark and one of the Masonic messengers was murdered. This Freemason code in the dollar bill remains part of some unfinished pyramid, and it contains a code that has apparently allegedly been passed down for generations among Freemasons, including people who were on the Air Force flight that crashed in the Andes in 1972, and Ted Bundy's escape from prison in 1977 that put him on a killing spree in Chicago, and now the flight that just crashed in our mountains and, get this, the murderer that just escaped from the Wyoming State Pen. My paralegal thinks that this is all related."

Burg stopped unpacking the food. He looked at his wife sideways. She was pregnant, so he knew from his past experiences with a pregnant hormonal wife to tread carefully. He did not know how to respond. It sounded outlandish.

"What do you think about this," Burg asked. It was a safe passage under the circumstances. He continued to serve her the shrimp and the sauteed beans. He served himself the sweet and sour chicken and the beans. He did not want to question her. She had a long day and they just found out that they were having a baby boy. He wanted to end on a high note.

Chapter 7

A document known as the "Unfinished Pyramid" was central to the Masonic rituals, and its design influenced the layout of symbols on the dollar bill. The murder at the 1910 baseball game was over possession of this document, and now, after the 1972 Air Force airplane crash, one of the survivors of the plane crash was in possession of it – unknowingly holding the key to a dangerous secret.

Mac was now very intrigued. She had a serious plane crash in her mountains and a convicted escaped murder on the loose, and somehow, all of these incidents were converging.

The more she investigated, the more she learned that the "Unfinished Pyramid" was to reveal a plan for a new world order, orchestrated by rogue Masonic renegades, and the escape in 1977 of serial killer Ted Bundy was part of this group. Nothing would stop these Masonic rogues from retrieving the blueprint and carry out their plans.

Chapter 8

The Masons' influence reaches far deeper than Mac imagined. The 1910 "life or death baseball game" at the Wyoming State Penitentiary, coupled with the 1972 Air Force crash in the Andes, and the 1977 prison break of serial killer Ted Bundy confluence as rituals of sacrifice and survival. Each event was allegedly part of a larger puzzle meant to test the loyalty of the Masonic society's members. Symbols on the dollar bill were clues left behind for those who were worthy of unlocking the ultimate prize: control over a powerful force that could shape the future. Mac would need to decipher these symbols and uncover how they could tie into a hidden Masonic agenda that could alter the course of history. But this was just the tip of the iceberg.

It turned out that this also might involve "The Secret" which was an Old World for the New World, involving 12 hidden treasures where were ceramic casques buried across North America, containing a key to the Masonic New World Order. Three had been identified. One in Chicago in 1984, another in Cleveland in 2004, and the third in Boston in 2019. Wyoming had the remaining nine.

Chapter 9

Mac was up all night with the Google researching what was a fantastical book by Byrom Preiss called "The Secret" published in 1982, with contributions from Ted Mann and Sean Kelly. The book included twelve cryptic verses and twelve detailed paintings, each pair hinting at the location of a buried casque. Solvers of this puzzle were to interpret the clues in the embedded artwork and the verses to find the exact burial spot of each casque.

Over the years, this treasure hunt captivated many puzzle enthusiasts, though only a few casques had been discovered to date.

The small ceramic containers buried in secret locations across North America hold a key that could be exchanged for one of twelve jewels: a sapphire, emerald, diamond, opal, ruby, and other precious stones. These jewels were chosen or their symbolic significance and were promised as rewards for those who could solve the riddles in the book and locate the casques.

The treasures were connected to the mythical migration of magical creatures from the Old World (Europe, Asia, and Africa) to the New World (North America). According to the fantasy storyline, fairies, goblins, leprechauns, and other mythical beings traveled across the ocean to escape the encroaching human presence in their original homelands.

As part of their journey, they buried these casques in significant locations in the New World, intending them to remain hidden.

Each of the twelve paintings in the book corresponds to one of these treasures and offers a wealth of symbolic clues related to the casque's location. Paired with a verse, these cryptic puzzles needed to be deciphered to pinpoint a specific spot in a city of a natural landscape where the casque was buried. To date, only three of the twelve casques have been found.

The Chicago, Illinois casque was found in 1983 in Grant Park near the Chicago Art Institute. This casque was associated with a ruby. The Cleveland, Ohio casque was discovered in 2004 in the Greek Cultural Garden and corresponded to an emerald. The Boston, Massachusetts casque was found in 2019 at the home plate of the former Boston Braves baseball stadium in Franklin Park, containing a key for an aquamarine.

Mac imagined that the nine remaining casques if buried in Wyoming, would likely be in a location rich in history, natural beauty, and cultural significance since each casque was hidden in a place tied to both local history and the fantastical creatures from the Old World mythology.

After giving it thought at four in the morning after a few cups of Moroccan Mint tea (recommended by her doctor in lieu of coffee while pregnant), she came up with some probable locations.

Yellowstone National Park was one of the most iconic natural landmarks in the United States. Containing geothermal features such as Old Faithful and the Grand

Prismatic Spring, both symbolizing mystical forces of nature. The area is also rich in wildlife and historical lore, with Native American mythology woven into the land's identity.

Devils Tower is a stunning, ancient geological formation in northeastern Wyoming and holds spiritual significance for many Native American tribes. Its otherworldly appearance is a perfect fit for mythical creatures to bury a casque. The name "Devils Tower" alone evokes a sense of mysticism and wonder. If a casque were buried here, clues might reference its unique shape, the native legends surrounding it, or the towering figure of the monolith.

Grand Teton National Park and the Tetons are a dramatic mountain range, with peaks that tower over the valley caldera floor, surrounded by lush forests and lakes. The park's serene beauty and awe-inspiring mountains make it a fitting place for a treasure hidden by mythical creatures fleeing to the New World. Clues might reference the jagged peaks or Jackson Lake, a glacial lake nestled below the mountains.

Fort Laramie National Historic Site is at a crossroads of Western history and a key location during the westward expansion and was visited by settlers, Native Americans, and trappers. A verse might allude to the site's role in history, referencing treaties, military activity, or the nearby Oregon Trail.

Buffalo Bill Center of the West in Cody, Wyoming is a museum complex in the legacy of the Wild West. With its focus on Western folklore and Native American history, the center could be tied to mythical themes alluding to Buffalo Bill's famous persona, the spirit of adventure, or the cultural blending of the Old and New Worlds.

The Fremont County Petroglyphs include carvings made by indigenous peoples, representing another layer rich in history and mystery. Clues might hint to ancient symbols or refer to the artwork on the stone faces, blending Native American heritage with mythical lore.

Medicine Wheel National Historic Landmark located in the Bighorn National Forest above Sheridan, Wyoming, is an ancient sacred Native American site, thought to have been used for religious or ceremonial purposes. It has spiritual and astronomical significance, with its wheel-like structure often compared to Stonehenge. A casque could be buried here, with a verse referencing the alignment of stars, the spiritual significance of the reverent place, and the circular layout of the stones.

Independence Rock, known as the "Register of the Desert," is a large granite rock and a landmark for pioneers traveling the Oregon Trail. Many carved their names into the rock, making it a historical and cultural symbol of the westward journey. Clues could include possibly pointing to the names etched in stone or the importance of the rock to travelers.

Pumpkin Buttes, similar to Devils Tower, but located in the Powder River Basin, is a spiritual landmark of three monoliths and worshiped by Native American tribes. It is known to contain uranium and three rare earth elements: Neodymium, Praseodymium, and Dysprosium. These rare earth elements are important for enhancing the performance of neodymium-based magnets, especially in high-temperature environments. This makes it crucial as electric motors and generators.

The Pumpkin Buttes could be prominent for the burial of casques linking the Old and New World.

Wyoming was the setting for these nine unfound treasures. Mac was learning of this for the first time. Burg, who was a native of Wyoming, had never heard of this mythology, nor had he heard of anything that she had disclosed in the past 24 hours. Was this pregnancy brain? Or was his brilliant wife onto something that others were unlikely to discover?

Chapter 10

Little known facts about the Wild West. When men drove wagons across the West, either to transport passengers or freight, or both, they often took another man to sit next to him and this man carried a shotgun for safety. This later became the modern shout-out when someone wanted to sit in the front passenger seat of a car.

Another little-known fact is that when a man was short on cash and wanted a drink at a local saloon, he would offer a bullet in exchange for usually a small glass of whiskey. The latter would become a "shot of whiskey."

The Wild West was wild, but literal as well. This made the mystical fairytale of casques hard to digest in Wyoming. People were honest, trustworthy, and literal.

But there exists a culture of mystique in Native Americans, and their beliefs date back for centuries of incredibly rich and unique traditions, beliefs, and values of hundreds of distinct indigenous tribes across North America. Each tribe has its own set of stories, spiritual beliefs, and practices that have been passed down through generations. However, there are some common themes that run through many Native American cultures.

Many Native American tribes emphasize a deep connection to the natural world. Nature, animals, and elements like the sun, moon, and stars often play central roles in their spiritual practice. The Earth is often seen as a living being, and all living creatures are considered part of a greater whole, interdependent, and sacred.

Ceremonies, dances, and rituals often honor this connection to nature. For example, the Hopi people perform ceremonies like the Snake Dance to pray for rain and harmony with nature.

Storytelling is an integral part of Native American culture, used not only for entertainment but also to teach moral lessons, history, and values. These stories are passed down orally, often with elders serving as keepers of the tribe's history and knowledge.

Myths and legends often feature trickster figures like Coyote or Raven, who play the role of both creator and troublemaker, teaching lessons through their mischief and cunning.

Many Native American tribes use totes – sacred symbols or animals that represent clans, families, or individuals. The totem may be seen as a spiritual protector and a symbol of identity.

Animals hold special symbolic meanings in Native American beliefs. For example, the eagle often represents strength and wisdom, while the wolf symbolizes loyalty and family.

Creation stories vary widely among tribes but often feature the Earth as a mother figure and animals as crucial participants in creation. For the Iroquois tribe, the world began on the bank of a tortoise. This motif of the "turtle island" is common in many northeastern tribes.

Other tribes like the Navajo have stories of emergence from underground worlds, symbolizing spiritual evolution and the journey of people.

Many Native American cultures believe in a supreme creator, often referred to as the Great Spirit or Wakan Tanka among the Lakota. This being is seen as the source of all life and is sometimes represented as both male and female or beyond gender.

Medicine men or women play a crucial role in healing and spiritual guidance within many tribes. They serve as intermediaries between the spiritual and physical worlds, using rituals, herbal medicine, and spiritual knowledge to help people heal. Often, the use of a sweat lodge, a sacred ritual used for purification, healing, and spiritual renewal, is used for many Native American tribes and involves essentially what would be considered a modern-day steam room inside of a native tent.

Shamans often engage in vision quests, ceremonies, and the use of sacred objects to communicate with spirits or heal the sick. These spiritual leaders hold immense respect in their communities.

Many Native American tribes have ceremonies to mark important life events or seasonal cycles, such as birth, puberty, marriage, and death. For example, the Sun Dance of the Plains tribes is a sacred ceremony that involves fasting, dancing, and sometimes self-sacrifice to ensure the well-being of the tribe. Other ceremonies, such as the Peyote Ritual involve the use of peyote, a sacred cactus, to connect with the divine spirit.

Folklore includes stories about the creation of the world, the deeds of gods and heroes, and the relationship between humans and animals.

For example, the Cherokee have stories about the Thunder Beings, who are responsible for rain and storms, while the Ojibwe speak of Nanabozho, a trickster figure who shaped the world forming what was originally Pangea.

Some legends serve as cautionary tales, teaching lessons about morality, respect for nature, and the importance of community.

Other tales involve strange behaviors that accompany a full moon, which is why some people are referred to as "lunatics" as the word "luna" means moon.

Humorously, back in the day, people would exchange a burlap sack of piglets for money, but if one was shy of a piglet, a kitten would be substituted, hence the saying, "Let the cat out of the bag."

In old-school boxing matches, they often began with a gentleman dropping his hat. Thus, the phrase, "at the drop of a hat" was born.

Continuing down this path, early century hat makers used mercury in the making of felt, and prolonged exposure to mercury caused workers to have tremors, personality changes, and erratic behavior, hence the term "mad as a hatter."

In early 20th century carnivals, cigars were given out as prizes and when a winner fell short, the phrase became, "close, but no cigar." In the same time period, in dimly lit environments, master craftsmen needed lighting and therefore, they used an apprentice to hold a candle nearby and when the apprentice fell short, the phraseology was "he couldn't hold a candle" to others.

Chapter 11

Mac accompanied Burg up the mountains to the scene of the plane crash. As they neared the coordinates of the crash site, Mac noted the desolate and dramatic area and she contrasted the snow-covered landscape with the wreckage of the aircraft.

The mountainous region was rugged and jagged with areas blanketed in snow, while other areas had begun the spring thaw revealing patches of spring greenery juxtaposed against bare exposed rocks. The sky was a mix of gray clouds with occasional beams of sunlight piercing through.

The snow, while thawing in some spots, was deep and pristine in others, making the crash site starkly visible. Debris was scattered across the white snow, with pieces of fuselage creating jagged, dark scars across the landscape.

The airplane, broken into multiple sections, appeared to have skidded down the slope and left behind a wake of dirt, broken pine tree branches, and oil-stained snow that almost had the appearance of blood. The pine trees surrounding the wreckage were snapped or burned from the impact, adding a tone of isolation.

The silence of the mountains made the scene even more eerie, with only sounds of mother nature with a light breeze, birds chirping nearby, and the occasional squirrel jumping from branch to branch in search of springtime nibbles.

Most notably, and the reason that Mac and Burg were on the scene, was that all survivors were accounted for, but one.

One man listed on the manifest was not recovered as a victim and did not present himself to the search, rescue, and recovery team. His footsteps, once detected by the team, had vanished from Mother Nature. He was missing, either by accident or by choice, and it was their job to figure out why.

Chapter 12

The Great Seal of the United States featured on the back of the U.S. dollar bill, contains a pyramid with an all-seeing eye at its top, known as the "Eye of Providence." The pyramid itself represents strength and endurance, and the unfinished state symbolizes that the nation is still growing. The Eye of Providence is thought to represent divine guidance or the favor of God watching over the nation.

Some theorists suggest that the Freemasons had influence over the design of the Great Seal and the U.S. dollar bill. This belief arises because the Eye of Providence, and some symbols used by Freemasons, are very similar. Freemasonry uses symbols like the all-seeing eye and pyramids, but there is no documented evidence that Freemasons were directly involved in the design of the Great Seal or the dollar bill. The Founding Fathers, some of whom were Masons, likely chose the symbols based on classical ideas, but many believe that these men were strongly influenced by their Freemason brethren.

The pyramid on the dollar bill is accompanied by the Latin phrases "Annuit Coeptis" which translates to "he favors our undertaking," and "Novus Ordo Seclorum, meaning "new order of the ages." Some people interpret these phrases as evidence of a secretive agenda tied to the Freemasons, while others believe that they were meant to reflect the birth of a new nation.

Chapter 13

Ted Bundy, one of the most notorious serial killers in American history, managed to escape from custody not once, but twice, both in Colorado in 1977. These escapes occurred due to a combination of several factors, including a lack of proper supervision, a lack of proper security measures, and Bundy's clever and cunning ability to manipulate situations.

His first escape occurred on June 7, 1977, from the Aspen Courthouse in Colorado's famous ski town. During a preliminary hearing for the murder of Caryn Campbell in Aspen, he was acting as his own defense attorney, which allowed him certain privileges such as access to legal books and materials and the ability to move more freely than a typical inmate. He was allowed to appear in court without restraints also, and this freedom gave him the chance to make a run for it while being inadequately supervised during a court recess. During this recess, he was allowed to visit the courthouse library under the guise of needing to look something up, and in doing so, he seized the opportunity to escape by jumping out of a second-story window and landing on his feet on the ground beneath him. He kept himself in good physical condition, which allowed him to outrun the law for six days while on the lam. He was caught driving a stolen vehicle in Aspen.

The second escape took place on December 30, 1977, from the Garfield County Jail in Glenwood Springs, Colorado. At this juncture, he was awaiting trial for this same murder and his escape plan was clever and calculated and exploited prison weaknesses in Colorado at the time.

Similar to the first escape six months' prior, the jail had improper security measures in numerous ways, including a flawed jail cell ceiling design. Similar to the escape from Alcatraz in 1962, Bundy painstakingly dug out a hole in the ceiling of his cell and was able to make good progress by stacking books and papers in his bed to look like he was asleep. He deliberately lost weight in order to make it easier for him to fit through the small access to a crawl space above the jail cells. On the night of his escape, there was no one closely monitoring Bundy, which gave him the freedom to move through the ceiling crawl space, access a jailer guard's apartment, and steal civilian clothing. Once changed, he simply walked out of the jail. His escape went unnoticed for hours, giving him adequate time to run.

He made his way to Chicago, and then on to Tallahassee, Florida, where he committed the brutal Chi Omega sorority house murders in January 1978. He was arrested in February 1978 in Pensacola, Florida, and was eventually convicted of murder.

Both prison escapes mirrored the escape that Mac and Burg were currently investigating regarding the man who escaped from the Wyoming State Penitentiary. This man also dug a hole in this old state prison and was able to walk out in plain sight wearing a guard's clothing left carelessly in the laundry facility onsite. This prison, by the name of Timothy Balleck, was sentenced to life without parole for the brutal rape and killing of a 14-year-old girl from Rock Springs, Wyoming. It was well-known that Timothy Balleck was a direct descendent of "Laughing Sam" Carey, a notorious figure and member of the Tipton Gang who was a participant in the "life or death baseball game" at the Wyoming State Penitentiary in 1910.

"Laughing Sam" Carey was a known member of the Freemasons and it was said that he was one of the keepers of the "secret code" and that he was championed with the mission to keep the secret alive by passing it down to his son and his son's son. Timothy Balleck. Now an escaped prisoner on the lam and rumored to be in or around Sheridan, Wyoming.

Mac and Burg were on the lookout for this man, who was highly identifiable by the teardrop tattoos on his face and his missing incisors.

Chapter 14

The Tipton Gang from the 1900s in Wyoming was a compilation of gangsters. The leader of the group was Eli Tipton and he was a key figure in organizing the gang's criminal activities. He was known for his strategic planning of robberies and evading law enforcement for years before being caught.

Frank Tipton was Eli's brother and was also heavily involved in the gang's activities. He acted as a second-in-command and helped coordinate their criminal operations.

Tom O'Day was a famous associate of the Tipton Gang. O'Day was also connected with Butch Cassidy and the Hole-in-the-Wall gang. He was involved in various robberies, including the train and stagecoach heists.

Bill McCoy was another member and was known for his expertise in cattle rustling. His knowledge of the Wyoming plains made him a valuable asset to the gang when it came to escaping the law.

"Laughing Sam" Carey was a notorious gang member and a prominent figure in Wyoming's outlaw circles, known for his dark sense of humor. He participated in a series of robberies alongside the Tipton Gang before eventually being captured.

The gang operated at a time when Wyoming was still part of the Wild West, and they took advantage of the remote, often lawless, areas to carry out their crimes. Law enforcement eventually caught up with the Tipton Gang, and many of its members were either arrested or killed in ambush shootouts.

Their story is intertwined with the broader history of outlaw gangs in Wyoming and the American Wild West.

Of the members of the Tipton Gang, "Laughing Same" Carey was a known member of the Freemasons, and he was a leader among them when not in prison. It is alleged that he did play in the 1910 "life or death baseball game" at the Wyoming State Penitentiary and it is rumored that his team won, resulting in him not being executed. Rather, folklore has it that during this game, which was said to be a ruse for a Freemason meeting, Laughing Sam escaped prison, carrying with him a "secret code" that would, in time, reveal a secret society spanning generations.

Chapter 15

In medieval times, people made a meal that was commonly referred to as "pudding" which involved using essentially a sausage casing and stuffing it with whatever scraps or leftovers existed in the house and it was never a consistent recipe. It varied from household to household depending on what was left over from other meals. No one knew what the pudding would taste like until they tried it. Hence, the colloquialism, the "proof is in the pudding." One needed to experience it to know how it turned out.

Mac and Burg had a conference call with the warden of the Wyoming State Penitentiary regarding the escaped inmate and the rumors that he could be hiding in the vicinity of Sheridan. The Warden wasn't positive of where Timothy Balleck was heading, but other inmates with whom Balleck had confided suggested that he was heading north towards the Bighorn mountains as he said that there existed a secret treasure buried in a specific location and made mention of a hidden casque with a very valuable jewel inside.

According to others in the prison, Balleck was often found in the library reading Freemason history and the use of symbolism to crack ancient codes. Balleck was convinced that his grandfather, who was part of the Tipton Gang and who survived the 1910 deadly baseball game at the state prison passed down this legend through other family members. Balleck told other inmates that he was heading to the burial spot and would uncover the casque, sell the treasure on the black market, and live out his days as a free, rich man.

People weren't sure what to believe, but they unanimously agreed that Balleck was strong in his conviction regarding the secret casque and the Masonic secret code, as he spoke of it often and researched it constantly.

When Mac and Burg hung up the phone, they got to work researching this concept to try to figure out if this treasure hunt could be true, they would need to narrow the scope of the burial area and send out search teams to canvas the mountains.

They had to keep in mind that there was another strange coincidence in the same area in the mountains of a man who walked away from an airplane crash and vanished into thin air.

There was a distinct possibility that both men were lurking in the mountains, and this could be dangerous. Timothy Balleck was a convicted murderer and the guy on the plane was from South America. They were completely unrelated in character, but it did seem odd that they were both mysteriously in the same area at the same time.

Chapter 16

In Tudor England, women wore their hair pinned up and this was not always comfortable as the pair was pulled tightly and the pins poked the scalp. When they returned home and were in private, they would unpin their hair to relax with the freedom of not having the annoyance of poking pins. Hence, the old saying, "Let your hair down," which means to relax or enjoy oneself.

Mac quickly realized that there was growing tension in town with the rumors flying that an escaped murderer was roaming freely among them. She had approved a search team under Burg's command and Burg had his best friend Stan on the lookout in a helicopter above the Bighorn mountains.

The more she and her paralegal researched these mysterious casques, of which there were allegedly 12 in North America with only three of them discovered to date, she realized that this escaped prisoner was searching for one likely containing a precious gem.

The most precious three gems included Tanzanite which is a violet-blue gemstone that is 1,000 times rarer than diamonds. It is only found in a small area near the base of Mount Kilimanjaro in Tanzania. The next in line is the pink diamond which is a rare and valuable variety of diamond that is more difficult to find than other fancy diamonds. The Pink Star diamond is the most famous specimen and is worth over $83 million. Last, but not least, is the Kyawthuite which is the rarest mineral on Earth, with only one known crystal found in Myanmar. It is a small, deep orange gemstone.

Other rare gemstones include red beryl which is only found in the Wah Wah Mountains of Utah.

Another is the black opal which is only found in Australia and features vivid colors against a black background. The Kashmir sapphire is mainly housed in museums and private collections. The Alexandrite is a chrysoberyl mineral that can change color depending on the light source and viewing angle. The Grandidierite is a pleochroic gemstone that can appear blue, green, or white depending on the light. The Benitoite is a rare blueish-purplish stone that can sell for up to $2,000 per carat.

Mac discovers that one of these rare gemstones could be a buried treasure in the mountains and that Timothy Balleck was on a hunt to unearth it.

Chapter 17

The term "rule of thumb" has several historical backings, but the earliest is found in the writing of James Durham, Church of Scotland minister in 1658, and essentially refers to the scientific manner in which a task is completed.

Both the Freemasonry symbols on the dollar bill and the clues from the book "The Secret" rely heavily on symbolic interpretation. The visual riddles of "The Secret" may have drawn inspiration from historical codes like those associated with Freemasonry, especially since both require deep insight into American history, culture, and geography.

Freemasonry is known for its use of geometry and symmetry in its symbolism. Similarly, some treasure hunters speculate that the locations of the casques are positioned in geometric patterns across the United States such as star shapes or compass designs. The hidden Freemason symbols on the dollar bill, particularly the pyramid and compass motifs, could have inspired similar patterns in "The Secret."

Freemasonry has long been tied to various conspiracy theories about hidden knowledge and secret societies guarding treasures or secrets. The novel taps into this cultural fascination with hidden treasures and long-lost relics, adding another layer of mystique by using cryptic poems and artworks. It's possible that the same allure of hidden truths and treasures links both phenomena in a metaphorical way.

Some believe that Freemasonry symbols are connected to secret maps hiding within U.S. symbols or documents.

This could feasibly be the connection of the exact locations on maps, which could theoretically be in the geometric shape of a star or compass and could be the treasure map that Timothy Balleck bragged about knowing while he was in prison.

Now that he was on the lam likely somewhere in the Bighorn mountains above Sheridan, Mac was keenly aware that he was a dangerous criminal and that he was on a mission to uncover a buried treasure in the form of a casque containing a rare and precious gem.

Chapter 18

In the old West, a "bit" was a form of currency wherein eight bits were equivalent to one dollar. Therefore, one bit was little, and it is where the phrase "a little bit" comes from.

Back in the day, emigrants from Greece when arriving on U.S. soil often worked the dockyard unloading cargo from ships. If the cargo appeared undamaged, the Greeks would agree that it was "Ala Kala" which in Greek means "OK" which is where the phrase "everything is okay" stems from.

In the old West, a cocktail was a type of horse that had a tail that pointed upward, which meant that it was not a purebred, or that it was "mixed" and that is why in modern terms a mixed drink is referred to as a "cocktail."

Mac and Burg were on the phone with Stan who was on his cell phone in the search and rescue helicopter looking for not one, but two men in the Bighorn mountains. Snow was melting in the springtime, and it did not allow Stan and his team to spot tracks in the snow. He had come up empty three days in a row, and having no answers for the residents of Sheridan as to the whereabouts of this escaped murderer was not sitting well with the constituency or Mac and Burg.

For Mac, everything was "a little bit" hazy, and it was not "okay" and despite her pregnancy, she was craving a "cocktail." She would have to settle on peppermint tea.

Chapter 19

There exists an Ancient Greek antidote written about by Pliny the Elder's Naturalis Historia wherein he describes that an antidote to poison always includes a grain of salt. This led to the idea that threats involving poison could be taken less seriously, or "with a grain of salt". Not everything should be accepted at face value and a certain degree of doubt was wise.

When Mac was researching this possible motive for Timothy Balleck's escape from the Wyoming State Penitentiary, he was on a mission to unearth a casque thought to have been buried somewhere in the Bighorn mountains. This treasure hunt is said to involve solving puzzles that line the twelve cryptic paintings with twelve verses in the book "The Secret". Each painting allegedly contains visual clues, and each verse provides poetic hints. The key is to correctly pair the right painting with the right verse, as each pair corresponds to a specific location in a city or place.

Both the paintings and the verses are filled with symbols and references to mythology, history, landmarks, or geography. For example, some images may feature architectural elements or numbers that hint at specific landmarks. The paintings often include subtle maps or details like shapes resembling states or famous monuments. The verses, on the other hand, contain directional clues that lead to precise locations.

Often the clues require knowledge of local history, cultural sites, or monuments. For example, a specific fountain or statue might be referenced in a way that only someone familiar with the area could recognize.

After matching the pair and interpreting the clues, hunters of these treasures can narrow the search to a specific park or public area. The verses and paintings often describe the final location in a step-by-step fashion that leads to a precise digging spot.

Since the story goes that the casques were buried in public places, often parks, it's important to get proper permission before excavation.

A famous example is the casque found in 2004 in Chicago's Grant Park, where hunters connected a painting's image to the park's skyline and landmarks, then used the verse to pinpoint the exact digging sport near the base of a fixture.

This process had Mac curious, but also skeptical. Was this really a thing that people did and was there truly a valuable item within the ceramic casque? She was not convinced, and she decided to "take it with a grain of salt".

Chapter 20

It was common knowledge that Timothy Balleck's troubled life was marked by trauma, instability, and growing desperation. His early life started on the outskirts of Rock Springs, Wyoming, a town known for drugs and crime. He was born to parents of poverty and substance abuse and it was not long before he was from a broken home His father had been a career criminal as had his grandfather and great-grandfather, and his heritage tied him to the Tipton Gang of cattle rustlers who served time at the Wyoming State Penitentiary and were part of the "life or death baseball game" of 1910.

Balleck grew up feeling isolated, with limited access to positive role models or opportunities for success. By adolescence, he was already acting out at a high level, failing school, struggling with anger management, and becoming involved in minor crimes such as theft and vandalism and eventually substance abuse. His disconnection from family, school, and community pushed him further into these margins. He spends time in juvenile detention, fostering a growing sense of resentment toward authority and society as a whole.

By the time he reached early adulthood, he joined a gang involving the illegal drug trade in order to survive. His anger and frustration led to violent outbursts, and a single moment of unchecked rage resulted in murder. A drug deal gone bad that escalated into a gun battle.

Being sentenced at age 20 to the Wyoming State Penitentiary did not help matters. Instead of finding rehabilitation, he grew more hardened and embittered.

His time in prison was filled with conflict – fighting with other inmates, pushing back against guards, and, ultimately, plotting his escape.

By the time he escaped in 2024, he had nothing to lose, living on survival instincts alone, planning revenge against those he blamed for his downfall while trying to stay ahead of the law while evading capture.

The Bighorn Mountains were a perfect refuge for him as a means to this end of revenge and evading capture. Plus, he was determined to find the buried casque and show the world how smart he was after all.

Chapter 21

Mac and Burg did not participate in the country club life that existed in Sheridan, Wyoming. There were ranchers and farmers who tended to be hard workers and social among themselves. There was also a hint of the dare-wells, some faction of criminal life that exists pretty much everywhere. But there was a large faction of well-off folks in this area. Some did well elsewhere and chose this idealistic location in a tax-free state for retirement. Others were professionals of whatever nature that tended to belong to the country club and played golf and tennis and such.

Mac and Burg did not fit into any of these factions. Mac was a professional, and Burg was a sheriff. They tended after work to be together exercising in nature and cooking together at home. It was not that they were antisocial people by any means, but that their jobs required constant interaction with others, and they both needed their respective downtime.

An exception to this rule was the Wyoming Business Alliance Annual Forum.This event focused on business development, public policy, and economic development and growth in Wyoming. It attracts professionals from a wide variety of fields, including healthcare, law, energy, and more, making it an ideal networking opportunity for high-level professionals.

Mac came down the staircase in a beautiful Mac Duggal dress that she found second-hand on a website. It was white and flowing with an intricate artistic sketch of women in artful poses. It was unique and matched her personality.

When Burg took one look at her, he said, "You are wearing a full nine yards of fabric!" Mac looked at him quizzically, wondering if the dress was ill-fitting or something of the like.

"I don't get it," she responded.

"Haven't you heard the phrase, 'you are dressed to the nines?'", he asked.

"Of course I have"

"This phrase comes from the olden days when wealthy people could afford to buy a full nine yards of fabric in order to   make   a   dress."

"Oh! So this is a compliment?" she asked.

"Yes, gorgeous wife of mine. It is a high compliment."

Chapter 22

Fellow passengers and crew from the plane that crashed in the Bighorns agreed that the man who disappeared on foot after the crash was in his mid-50s and had a rugged, weathered appearance, suggesting years of exposure to harsh environmental conditions. The passenger log listed him from Peru with the name of Juan Lopezsanchez. His passport listed him from Lima, the capital of Peru. And his photograph depicted a man with dark, sun-kissed skin with salt and pepper thick hair, and tied back in a ponytail, with a thick, well-kept beard. He wore a wide-brimmed hat on the tarmac but took it off on the plane.

He wore cargo pants of a dark nature, sturdy boots, and a worn leather jacket with plenty of pockets. He had a backpack and wore a necklace of turquoise and silver in what appeared to be indigenous symbols.

One crew member said that she recalled a sense of grit or determination in his eyes. He spoke to no one.

Chapter 23

Burgess Junction is a scenic mountain pass located in the heart of the Bighorn Mountains of Wyoming. Sitting at an elevation of about 8,000 feet, it serves as a crossroads for travelers on U.S. Routes 14 and 14A, offering a gateway into the rugged, picturesque terrain of the Bighorns, the landscape is characterized by expansive forests of pine and spruce, rolling alpine meadows, and jagged rock formations, with panoramic views stretching as far as the eye can see across the mountain range.

In the summer, the area is lush and green, dotted with wildflowers, and provides access to popular outdoor activities such as hiking, camping, fishing, and rock climbing. The area is ripe with streams and lakes, attracting outdoor enthusiasts and wild game such as moose, bear, elk, and deer.

In the winter, it transforms into a snowy wonderland, with attractive skiers, snowmobilers, and cross-country skiers.

Burgess Junction itself is relatively remote, with a few small lodges, cabins, and campgrounds that serve as a base for camps for adventurers. The wildlife in the area exudes a peaceful, rustic charm, making it a quiet yet pivotal stop for travels exploring the grandeur of the Bighorns.

The Medicine Wheel, located about 20 miles west of Burgess Junction, sits at an elevation of roughly 9,600 feet, on Medicine Mountain, and is a sacred Native American site. The road to the Medicine Wheel offers stunning views of the surrounding mountains, and visitors must hike a short distance from the parking area to reach the actual site.

The Medicine Wheel is an important cultural and historical site for many Native American tribes. It consists of a circular stone structure with spokes radiating from the center, resembling a wheel. Believed to have been built over a thousand years ago, it serves various purposes, including astronomical observations and ceremonial rituals.

The site is situated at a high elevation, offering breathtaking views of the surrounding landscape. It has become a popular destination for visitors interested in archaeology, history, and Native American culture. The Medicine Wheel is also associated with various legends and spiritual beliefs, adding to its mystery, allure, and significance.

One of the legends associated with the Medicine Wheel is that it is a site for one of the buried treasure casques containing a very valuable jewel inside.

The painting associated with "The Secret" is a Stonehenge-looking rock outcropping, but legend has it that these 12 casques were only buried in North America. One of the verses associated with this treasure hunt has a line that reads, "As the crow flies." The Crow Native Americans are the closest reservation in the Wyoming/Montana area and are within a reasonable distance from the Medicine Wheel, "as the crow flies."

Mac, after learning about Jose Lopezsanchez and deciphering from his background check that he was a known South American treasure trove seeker, was beginning to believe that perhaps he walked away from a plane crash in order to have access to the Medicine Wheel.

The cause of the crash was still under investigation, but some of the passengers and especially the crew felt like there was foul play involved.

The plane took off from Mexico City en route to Cody, Wyoming. It was a privately chartered jet, and the manifest listed the reservation under Aztec Inc., registered to do business in South America with headquarters in Lima, Peru.

Chapter 24

When Mac first moved from Jackson Hole to Sheridan, Wyoming, her former boss and mentor, Harry, came to visit her and wish her all the luck in the world. He was a father figure to her and they were extremely close.

He wanted to take her to a place where his parents had taken him as a kid, and the place was none other than Spear-O-Wigwam located in the Bighorn Mountains.

Spear-O-Wigwam is a historic lodge and camp area originally built in the 1920s and was a retreat for outdoor enthusiasts seeking to enjoy the rugged beauty of Wyoming's wilderness. Surrounded by dense forests, alpine lakes, and vast mountain landscapes, it offers a serene environment perfect for hiking, horseback riding, fishing, archery, and other outdoor activities.

The camp, which has been used for youth and adult retreats, combines rustic charm with the breathtaking scenery of the Bighorn Mountains, making it a special spot for those looking to disconnect and immerse themselves in nature.

It is also a place where it is highly possible that a casque was buried and it was growing plain to Mac that Timothy Balleck might be lurking in that area on a treasure hunt. It was springtime and long before the area was populated with folks who owned cabins there and tourists who came to stay, so it was a calculated opportunity to hunt for a treasure and remain undiscovered.

Chapter 25

Mac had to formulate a plan as to what she would do if the rumors were true, and more importantly, her speculations were real. If these two men were converging in the same area with the same quest, there could be serious trouble.

First and foremost, if both men were going for the Medicine Wheel, which was highly likely if any of this were true, they would be public enemy number one to each other. One was a known murderer. The other was on some strange U.S. Visa that allowed South American in the United States for three months without much of a plan. Mac had no clue what Juan Lopezsanchez was about, and why he wanted to fly to Cody, Wyoming.

She also knew that she knew nothing about prosecuting such a crime. Treasure-seeking in and of itself was not a crime. Gold prospectors had been doing this in the Wild West for centuries, and it was clearly not a crime to find precious metals that were not protected for whatever reason.

However, excavating from a protected area was a crime without specific permission from a number of sources, and it was her job to determine this ahead of time.

In tennis, when the ball is hit by the opponent, it is the responsibility of the opponent to keep the ball in play. It is the basis of the term, "The ball is in your court."

Mac knew that she had to get ahead of the ball, so that if this speculation that she had come to fruition, "the ball would be in her court." Literally and figuratively.

Chapter 26

Mac spent the weekend researching what the legal issues might include and she arrived at the conclusion that the specific crime would depend on the protection status of the site and the nature of the disturbance caused. Burg was covering for one of his deputies for the weekend, and this made working all weekend more bearable. She could do the research from home, and her rescue kittens loved her attention when she took breaks.

Her research revealed that the Medicine Wheel is a sacred site and is protected under several laws, such as the National Historic Preservation Act (NHPA_ and possibly the Archaeological Resources Protection Act (ARPA). Excavating and damaging this site could be a federal offense under these laws. Penalties for violating ARPA, for example, include fines of up to $250,000 and imprisonment for up to five years.

If the excavation took place without proper authorization, it could be considered trespassing, especially if the land is clearly marked as protected or off-limits.

The Medicine Wheel is a Native American sacred site and disturbed it could be considered desecration. Such an act might be subject to prosecution under laws protecting Native American heritage sites, including the Native American Graves Protection and Repatriation Action (NAGPRA), even if no human remains are involved. Fines or imprisonment could result from damaging sacred or historically significant landmarks.

Beyond criminal charges, there could be civil lawsuits from Native American tribes or government agencies seeking reparations for damage to the site. These suits could result in significant financial penalties.

Mac knew enough to know that these two men must have known what they were looking for when they set out on their quest, and they must have known what was at stake.

That alone gave her pause. This was dangerous. They both must know it.

She was new to this and behind the eight ball. She would need to get up to speed quickly and try to think in a manner they were thinking.

Folks like these two men studied this "folklore" which had turned out to be true in three cases as recently as 2019. There must be some truth in these buried treasures.

She was skeptical, but she knew that she had to swipe herself of skepticism and rely on the facts in order to prepare.

Chapter 27

Mac had a fitful night's sleep and kept going back into a reoccurring dream about losing their baby. She had felt little flutters in her tummy the day before and this must have been the impetus to her dream cycle.

She knew how much Burg wanted a baby boy and it did make her a little nervous. She didn't want to let him down. She was considered old for a first-time pregnancy, and she knew very little about her own mother and her experiences in pregnancy, so she did not know what to expect.

But as she awoke at her normal hour, she awoke after a different dream – this one involved Devils Tower in Wyoming.

Devils Tower is a striking geological formation located in northeastern Wyoming, and a national monument with significant cultural, historical, and spiritual significance.

Devils Tower is an ancient volcanic feature, rising 1,267 feet above the surrounding landscape and reaching an elevation of 5,112 feet above sea level. It's made of phonolite porphyry, a rare igneous rock, and was formed through the intrusion of magma millions of years ago. Over time, erosion of the softer surrounding rock exposed the harder columns of the Tower.

The Tower is characterized by its columnar jointing, a phenomenon where the lava cooled and fractured into hexagonal columns. These towering columns, some over 600 feet high, give the formative its distinctive appearance.

Native Americans believe that a giant bear tried to climb the monolith and the claws of the bear formed the columns of the Tower.

Devils Tower is a sacred site to many Native American tribes, including the Lakota, Cheyenne, Arapaho, Crow, and Kiowa. Numerous legends explain its creation, the most well-known being the Lakota story where the Tower was formed to protect two girls from this giant bear. The Tower raised up in this natural setting while the bear tried to kill them and it was the bear's claw marks that were etched into the sides of the rock during this encounter that formed this monument. The Tower is also known by several native names, such as "Bear Lodge" or "Bear's Tipi."

Many tribes continue to use the Devils Tower for prayer and rituals. Visitors may see prayer cloths tied to trees at the base of the Tower, left by Native American practitioners. These offerings are part of their ongoing spiritual connection to the land.

Devils Tower was declared the first U.S. National Monument by President Theodore Roosevelt in 1906. He was also the President to declare Yellowstone the first U.S. National Park on the northwestern side of the state of Wyoming. These designations help protect this land from commercial exploitation and preserve the natural and cultural heritage.

European-American explorers and settlers arrived in the region in the late 1800s. The first recorded ascent of the Tower was in 1893 by William Rogers and Willard Ripley, who used a wooden ladder to scale the formation. A section of the ladder remains visible today.

Devils Tower is a popular destination for rock climbing.

Its vertical cracks and columns provide unique climbing challenges. However, out of respect for Native American cultural practices, the National Park Service asks climbers to voluntarily refrain from climbing in June, a time of significant cultural ceremonies.

The surrounding landscape is rich in wildlife, including prairie dogs, which can often be seen in colonies at the base of the monument. Deer, eagles, antelope, and various other animals also inhabit the area.

"Close Encounters of the Third Kind" was filmed here and was a Steven Spielberg sci-fi film about human communication with extraterrestrial visitors. People still use the phrase, "E.T. phone home" when asking someone to call them.

Devils Tower is near the Belle Fourche River which meanders through the park and has historically been vital for both Native American and settler activity, providing water and supporting the local ecosystem.

The region is a mix of forests and grasslands, typical of the high plains environment. The area is home to a wide variety of flora, including ponderosa pine and various grass species.

It is also a place where there is mention that a casque might be buried due to its sacred nature.

Mac was completely focused on the Bighorn Mountains. This dream caused her to pivot. She called Burg at work and told him what she was thinking. Burg immediately called Stan and asked that he direct another search team to Devil's Tower to see if one of these men could possibly be in the vicinity searching for a treasure.

Chapter 28

As Mac awaited news from Burg, Stan, and the search teams on the ground and in the air, she continued her research into the Masonic symbolism in the ceramic casques allegedly buried in North America. Not only did many of the sites like the Medicine Wheel and Devil's Tower have similar symbolism, but they also aligned with Masonic symbolism like the compass, square, and the All-Seeing Eye on the U.S. dollar bill.

Mac asked a fellow attorney in town if he knew of any leaders in the local Masons group, and he explained that there was a scholar in the local Masons who was well-schooled in the old and new teachings of Freemasonry. His name was Donald Townsend, and she was offered his phone number at the bar that he owned downtown.

Mac had heard of the Rainbow Bar on Main Street, but she had never been in it. The only bar she had gone to a few times with Burg was the Last Chance Bar out in Big Horn, Wyoming. She popped into the Mint Bar in town for a quick drink with Burg once, as she knew that it was iconic in town and there was an old saying in Sheridan that went, "Meet you at the Mint." That was how friends greeted one another and socialized.

Mac dialed the number to the Rainbow Bar and a man answered, "This is Don." He answered his own business phone. That impressed her.

She introduced herself and explained that she was the town prosecutor and that she was investigating a plane crash in the mountains where a passenger walked away on foot, as well as an escaped murderer from the Wyoming State Penitentiary. Don was aware of who she was and the two men on the lam. One thing that was true of most bar owners, they knew the town gossip. Bartenders knew as much as hair stylists when it came to the local scoop.

After consulting with Donald Townsend, she started to theorize that the puzzles leading to the casques might hold dual meanings – one to locate the treasure, and another that could reflect deeper Masonic mysteries or ritualistic knowledge.

For example, a casque hidden near a statue or a monument could represent the Freemason principle of "building" or craftsmanship, with the alignment in relation to a local Masonic lodge or a structure significant to Freemason history.

As Mac continued to dig into the history of the Freemasons, she discovered that several characters from "The Secret" novel could have been central in organizing the treasure hunts and that these characters were all members of the Freemasons.

These people likely concealed certain symbolic meanings in the casques' location, Mac surmised. She was unsure of her theories, but after speaking with Donald Townsend and continuing her research, she felt like this outlandish notion might have some traction.

Chapter 29

Mac was notorious for writing down her theories and her trial briefs and opening and closing statements to the juries were epic. She was theatrical and believable, but she had to script every word. She could not adlib her thoughts, because she was known in conversation to go down dark rabbit holes. Her former boss and mentor, Harry, often stopped her short and directed her back to her desk to write and stop talking.

He was correct. So she kept writing her thoughts and added her research and she was growing more confident that the placement of the casques was part of an encrypted knowledge, either a means for revelation or perhaps to distract others from discovering more significant treasures hidden by the Masons.

She also suspected that there was a possibility that a criminal organization, possibly with Masonic ties, had been using the search for the casques to launder money or conceal some other illegal activity. She considered the notion that the treasure hunt was part of a public distraction, while a more sinister operation was in play. She thought that it could involve the illegal smuggling of artifacts could be happening behind the scenes. Where did these extremely rare gemstones or jewels come from? Most of what was written explained that these rare gems were from distant islands and continents and were very difficult to extract from Mother Earth. How would one organization get their hands on 12 of them, Mac wondered while writing down her thoughts.

And then she got the call from Burg who had patched in Stan who had made a gruesome discovery in the Bighorn Mountains.

There was a dead man found in a pool of blood near the Medicine Wheel. The kill was recent. There was a murderer in their midst.

Chapter 30

Burg sent his forensic team to the scene of the crime to investigate who had been murdered and to secure the site to gather evidence. Burg went with this team, and he was expected to be gone the rest of the day. He would miss Mac's ultrasound to confirm that the baby was thriving. Her dreams had a number on her psychologically, and when she told her OBGYN about them, her female physician insisted that an ultrasound would put her anxiety to rest.

It didn't take forensics long to discover that the dead man found adjacent to the Medicine Wheel was Juan Lopez-Sanchez from Peru. The man who was missing from the plane crash in the Bighorn Mountains from a few weeks prior.

Mac learned that Lopez-Sanchez was a wealthy treasure hunter, believed to be searching for one of the casques. Mac's suspicions were coming to fruition. She thought that maybe Lopez-Sanchez was getting too close to discovering the casque buried near the Medicine Wheel, and now she configured that it was Thomas Balleck who killed him. Balleck was a convicted murderer and a recent escapee from the Wyoming State Penitentiary where he spoke often of these casques and his ploy to find one and become rich. It was thought by the prison ward that Balleck would head to the Bighorn Mountains, as he bragged about it to fellow inmates.

The crazy part of what Mac learned from the Peruvian Consulate was that Lopez Sanchez was a known member of the Peruvian Freemasons.

Just when she thought that she could be onto something even bigger than a conspiracy, her phone rang. It was Donald Townsend, the owner of the Rainbow Bar and a well-known Freemason member and scholar. He called to tell her that he had made a few calls and a fellow Mason told him that there was a member of the Freemasons by the name of Michael MacIntosh.

Michael MacIntosh was Mac's deceased father.

Chapter 31

Mac grew up hearing the whispers of secret societies but always dismissed them as irrelevant – until now. Upon learning that her father and grandfather were part of the Freemasons threw in a wrench of a personal stake to her investigation. When Mac told Burg the news, he was astonished. He knew his wife all too well. This personal stake would drive her to a relentless pursuit of the truth.

Chapter 32

Burg called Mac and woke her to tell her that Stan was aerial spotting what his search team believed to be Thomas Balleck. As the spring temperature was rising but the foliage had not grown back on the Aspen and Maples, it made aerial surveillance good.

It wasn't like there was a blood trail or anything obvious. But the Medicine Wheel was at a high elevation where there was still a lot of snow, and his tracks were quite obvious from the air.

Stan and his team had narrowed the search to a very specific area and the tracks were heading due east. Toward Devil's Tower.

Chapter 33

"He desecrated Medicine Wheel and there are probably thirty holes that are dug. I can't tell if he found anything," Stan said to Burg and Mac from the air. "The deepest is where the crime scene tape remains where the dead body was."

"Let forensics deal with that," Burg said.

"We need to find him. Do you think he has access to a vehicle," Mac asked.

"We think he might. There aren't many ways to easily ascent the Bighorns on foot, so we think he is taking the Redgrade road, but Spear-O-Wigwam would be an easy way to steal a car. Many folks own a cabin there and many leave a vehicle up there for use. There are too many vehicles to narrow the search, so if you could put a PSA out, asking for help from anyone who might leave an SUV up there to please inform us what that might look like, that would help. Newer cars are hard to hotwire. Older cars, like Jeeps, are easy. If we knew what to look for, it would make the search easier."

"Consider it done," Burg said.

He was drinking coffee in bed next to Mac and she was listening on his cell phone. He had arisen early before sunrise and had her mint tea on her nightstand before she stirred. He had missed her ultrasound two days' prior that confirmed a healthy baby boy, and he wanted to take care of her at the highest level. The phone call had awakened her, and she sipped her tea had lavender honey and a slice of lemon, just like she preferred.

Burg called his ground search team to release an APB with a photograph of Timothy Balleck. His PBA would be on the morning radio in an hour.

Chapter 34

Anita Shamber responded to the PBA immediately and reported that her old Jeep Wagoneer was always left at Spear-O-Wigwam year-round. She had not been up the mountain since last fall, and she had no way of knowing its whereabouts, but she did agree that it was an older model, and most folks knew that older model cars were simple to hotwire. Especially for criminals.

Her Jeep was an unattractive dull brown with faux wood paneling from the 1970s and was distinctively dated.

Stan had his eyes on it within no time.

Chapter 35

Mac did not grow up with a sense of community, and Sheridan, Wyoming was all about community. She loved living here. She could not imagine living elsewhere.

Top it off is that she met the man of her dreams who liked to ski and hike and pickleball and camp and fish and the list was endless. They were soulmates and their baby boy was healthy despite her bad dreams.

Chapter 36

Mac was gravely concerned that not only her father, but her grandfather, and likely others in her family, were involved in this secret society. She talked with Burg about it late into the evening and he agreed that it was concerning. He wasn't aware of the secrets of this group and he was learning an earful from her about it. It was alarming.

More alarming to both of them was the fact that they had a murder scene at Medicine Wheel in the Bighorn Mountains and that a killer was for certain on the loose in the vicinity.

Mac had a press conference scheduled the next morning and she would make her PSA regarding the safety of citizens in the Sheridan, Wyoming area.

Burg had a similar press conference scheduled an hour after her with the same message.

Lock your doors. Stay vigilant. Schools were closed on this late Spring Friday. Kids need to be safely watched by caretakers, as this escaped murderer from the Wyoming State Penitentiary was on the loose and had just killed a man at the Medicine Wheel.

Mac and Burg were sure that he was the killer. They just did not know of his whereabouts.

Chapter 37

On October 16, 1889, Emma Howell Knight, future dean of women at the University of Wyoming, wed Wilbur Clinton Knight, future UW professor of mining and metallurgy parents of future longtime UW Geology Professor Samuel Howell Doc Knight.

Emma Howell Knight, the University of Wyoming's first dean of women, was born Elizabeth Emma Howell on August 24, 1865, in Millbrook, Ontario, Canada and when her family moved to Omaha, Nebraska when she was a young child, it was life-changing.

She attended the University of Nebraska, and this was where she met her future husband. She married Wilbur Knight on October 16, 1889, and moved to the Keystone mining district in the Medicine Bow Range about 35 miles southwest of Laramie, Wyoming, where the University of Wyoming exists.

There, Wiblur had already been working for two years as a mining engineer at the Florence mine. Their first child, Florence, was born in 1890 and named after the mine.

Emma and Wilbur had four children. Samuel, Everett, and Oliver their three sons in addition to Florence.

Emma was active in Laramie society and campus activities and she was secretary of a women's club in Laramie and played the organ during Sunday services at the Wyoming Territorial Prison.

In 1903 Wilbur died unexpectedly of a ruptured appendix, at the age of 44.

To support her four children, Emma ran and was elected to the position of Albay County superintendent of schools in 1904. The job required her to travel the county frequently, inspecting schools – by horse and buggy in the early years and later by automobile. Often she took her four children with her.

At the same time, she continued her undergraduate education, beginning at the University of Nebraska in Lincoln, Nebraska. She continued at the University of Wyoming in Laramie and graduated with her Bachelor of Science degree in the spring of 1911, which happened to be the same year that her daughter also graduated.

Emma Knight was appointed advisor of women and assistant head of home economics at the University of Wyoming in 1911, then she was promoted to assistant professor in 1913.

She was well thought of as a touter of thought and ideas and she spoke often regarding her dream that the dean of women should be the natural enemy of every male student.

In 1918 she became the University of Wyoming's first full-time dean of women, a post that she held until her retirement in 1920.

Emma died on September 24, 1928, at the age of 63, which was considered a full life at the time.

In 1941, the University of Wyoming named the new women's dormitory in her honor, Knight Hall, which currently holds administrative offices. Emma was buried at the Greenhill Cemetry in Laramie, Wyoming.

Wyoming was the first state in the Suffrage Movement to grant women the right to vote in the United States of America.

Wyoming was also one of the early states to grant a woman like Emma Knight a position as dean at the only university in the state.

Folks think of Wyoming as old-school. Wyoming was more progressive than New York or anywhere that the Ivy League are to this day.

Chapter 38

Mac and Burg were certain that Thomas Balleck would be digging for the casque at Medicine Wheel in the dark of night. Stan could not fly his helicopter in the dark. But Burg and his team, with Stan and his team, could be hiding in the vicinity of the Medicine Wheel, on the lookout for any sign of activity.

Dumb criminals are notoriously dumb. It is universal. Balleck was after one thing and he was not leaving empty-handed.

Chapter 39

Mac was set to appear in court that morning before Judge Maurita Redle for an arraignment of a methamphetamine dealer in Sheridan County. She could no longer fit in her suits and had not purchased maternity wear yet because she was convinced that the minute she did, something nefarious would happen.

She used a large safety pin to hold her skirt together and made her way to the courthouse.

Meanwhile, Burg, Stan, and the team remained on surveillance, and sure as the sunrise, Balleck appeared to desecrate the Medicine Wheel in his pursuit of the casque.

The team had agreed in advance to let him start digging before they would go in for the capture because Mac had instructed them that she wanted to prosecute him for this additional crime. She told them to allow a few shovel hits, but no true disturbance to this ancient and worshipped ceremonial grounds for Native Americans. She wanted the message to be crystal clear. Do not, under any circumstances, disturb anything ceremonial to Native Americans in Wyoming.

Chapter 40

The team swiftly and silently encircled Balleck. They filmed him desecrating the Medicine Wheel before they swooped in for arrest. He did not see them coming. Ninjas. They were well-trained by Burg.

He called his pregnant wife to report that they had Balleck in custody that they were bringing him down the mountain for booking, and that she would need to file charges before arraignment. She quickly had her paralegal do the pleadings, as she wanted to have arraignment the next morning before the judge.

He would not only be charged with murder and escape from a state prison but also with desecrating a state monument. Charges would stick, no question about it, but her concern was broad-scoped.

National media would have a field day with respect to the attempted unearthing of this casque. This one was thought to have the rare gemstone of Tanzanite. If true, treasure hunters from around the world would want a piece of this action.

She needed federal assistance to protect the Medicine Wheel. It was a historical landmark and precious to many Native American tribes.

As she had recently prosecuted a uranium case involving the illegal export of "yellowcake" to Russia from the Pumpkin Buttes of Wyoming, she had no problem getting the help that she requested to protect this state monument from treasure hunters, and she would have the privilege of prosecuting a known murderer for several crimes.

Chapter 41

Not only was Wyoming the first state to grant women the right to vote but is holds the first national park. Yellowstone National Park was established in 1872 and is the world's first national park and a significant symbol of the conservation movement.

Wyoming has the first national monument as well. In 1906, Devils Tower was designated as the first national monument by President Theodore Roosevelt.

In 1942, Wyoming elected the first female governor. Nellie Tayloe Ross became the first woman in the United States to be elected as a state governor.

In addition, in 1870, Wyoming was the first state to allow women to serve on a jury.

These milestones demonstrate Wyoming's pioneering spirit.

Chapter 42

"All rise," the bailiff announced as Judge Maurita Redle entered and took the bench. She shuffled the files in front of her before calling the first case.

"The People vs. Thomas Balleck," she announced with authority.

Mac stood and identified herself on the record as the prosecutor. Her skirt shifted when she stood, and she worried that the safety pin that she used to make her suit fit had somehow come loose. She needed to get maternity clothing the following weekend. Her pregnancy was progressing in a healthy way despite her bad dream.

Thomas Balleck was escorted by two deputies into the courtroom and was placed at the defendant's table. As this was his arraignment, he would need to be appointed an attorney.

"The court appoints you a public defender in the event that you have not secured private counsel," Judge Redle said.

"I don't need no attorney," Balleck said. "I can represent myself. You people will convict me no matter what," he said in a snotty tone.

"As much as I would like to allow you to represent yourself, Mr. Balleck, I will appoint you an attorney so that your appeal is less likely to be granted," the judge pronounced. "I appoint public defender Rodifer on your behalf.

Mac rolled her eyes. Her thought bubble would have read something like, "he is better off representing himself" but she did not voice her opinion out loud.

The public defender had been given notice that she would be appointed on this arraignment, but was not present, and as usual, late. Judge Redle had a busy docket and was not going to wait around for this public nuisance to show up. She was just reading the charges to the defendant and could forego asking for him to enter a plea of guilty or not guilty until he had counsel present.

"You are hereby charged with murder in the first degree, violation of the National Historic Preservation Act, the Archaeological Resources Protection Act, trespassing, and violation of the Native American Graves Protection and Repatriation Act. In addition, you are charged with escape from the Wyoming State Penitentiary. We will forgo a plea of guilt or not guilty if you have counsel present. This matter will be continued until tomorrow morning for that purpose," Judge Redle said.

Mac remained silent. Her charging papers were well drafted, and she didn't want to interrupt. She needed to get back to her office because she needed to use the restroom in the worst way. Her bladder seemed to be shrinking with every day of advancing pregnancy.

Balleck was her only case on Judge Redle's docket and as soon as he was safely escorted out of the courtroom, she made a mad dash out and raced to her office to use her private restroom.

After relieving herself and drinking more water, she called Burg to let him know that his prisoner was on his way back to the jail pending a further hearing the next morning. Burg had already heard from his deputies and was aware of the facts.

"I need to go shopping," Mac told him. My clothes no longer fit.

"Good," Burg said. "I will go with you. When do you want to go?"

"This weekend should work."

"Why don't we go now," Burg suggested. "I can take my lunch break early."

She was surprised by Burg's willingness to go shopping with her. He hated to shop even more than she did. She was also inwardly delighted and agreed to dart out for an hour and find some maternity wear that wasn't super frumpy. She had never purchased anything along these lines, and she figured that she would only be pregnant this one time. She was advanced in age for pregnancy and was considered high-risk. She didn't want to invest a lot of money in clothes that she would likely only wear for a few months.

Burg was not buying into this notion. He was convinced that she would have two children with him. He wanted to buy her some nice and comfortable outfits that she could wear to work, as well as athletic clothing for her fitness obsession. He had two daughters from his prior marriage and his former wife worked while pregnant, so he therefore was aware of maternity wear and wanted Mac to be comfortable at work and at play. He spent several hundred dollars ensuring that she looked smart.

Chapter 43

Mac's OBGYN asked her to come in for yet another ultrasound because her pregnancy measurements were off. She was getting too big too fast and she was not gaining much weight, so they wanted a blood sample to check for gestational diabetes and an ultrasound to get more accurate measurements.

Her lab came was normal. Her ultrasound was as well. They were expecting twin boys. Burg was over the moon.

Chapter 44

Mac submitted her trial brief in a timely manner as usual for the case pending against Thomas Balleck. Rosemary Rodifer, the public defender appointed on his behalf, did not submit a trial brief at all. Nor did she submit jury instructions or a witness list. It was pathetic.

It was time for Mac's opening statement to the jury. After Judge Redle took the bench and the jury was seated, Mac stood to deliver what she believed she could prove true.

"Ladies and gentlemen of the jury, the tale that I'm about to spin is not outlandish. I have researched it well and it is the truth. It may seem far-fetched, but I assure you that fact is often trickier than fiction," Mac started. She was wearing her knit maternity suit of a dark gray nature with a cotton blouse. She had a tendency to sweat during opening statements and she did not want to ruin yet another silk blouse.

"The murder that took place at the Medicine Wheel is part of a much larger crime. It involves an age-old conspiracy dating back centuries. The group involved will not surprise most of you. Most of you are aware of the Freemasons. There is a Masonic temple down the street. This conspiracy to commit murder involves the Freemasons, who have long held out a belief that the dollar bill contains a secret code. This in fact is true, but it goes far deeper than this. The Freemasons also believe that the casques that are buried in various places in North America, including the Medine Wheel in our local mountains, also contain a secret. This secret gives the Freemasons power and wealth.

Thomas Balleck is a Freemason and so were his father and his grandfather. Now, there is nothing wrong with being a Mason. Truth be told, my father and grandfather were also Masons. This is not about a judgment on Masons. It goes beyond this," Mac continued. She had the attention of everyone in the courtroom, especially the jurors.

"This treasure hunt for the casques, due to the nature of each casque containing rare jewels that are highly valuable, does provide power and wealth. But it is also part of a larger criminal enterprise. The Freemasons have used this treasure hunt for the casques to cover what they are really doing. They have used this treasure hunt to cover up their grand conspiracy to smuggle ancient artifacts into the United States."

There was an audible gasp in the courtroom. Mac knew that the jury was following her story. She turned on her computer projector and the screen lit up with a visual demonstration that tied these facts together.

Mac was very computer savvy and loved using technology in her courtroom presentations. It drove her points home succinctly and powerfully.

"I will proceed to the next screen which I will submit at this time into evidence as well, and you will have a copy of it during your deliberations. She toggled to public historical records, city archives, and expert interviews on Freemasonry and their secrets," she continued.

"This web of conspiracies pieces together how the casques' locations tie to Masonic secrets." She clicked to the next slide on her computer which was cast onto the courtroom screen in front of the jury.

"As you can see in this Venn diagram, these records converge to prove that the Freemasons funded the hiding of these casques in order to illegally smuggle ancient artifacts into this country."

Mac continued her opening statement. "How does this tie in with the murder of Mr. Lopezsanchez? Thomas Balleck was chosen by the Freemasons to commit this murder as they were afraid that Mr. Lopezsanchez was about to unearth the fourth casque that is buried at the Medine Wheel. This would have given the victim of this murder power and wealth and would have been a major setback to the Freemasons. They chose a man already on death row at the Wyoming State Penitentiary to murder him because it would not affect the outcome of Balleck's life. He was already serving a life sentence," she continued.

Mac continued to toggle computer screens. "The secret code that the Freemasons strongly believe in includes the symbols of the 'All-Seeing-Eye' on the dollar bill and the clues and puzzles surrounding the buried casques. This cannot be a coincidence. The symbols are too significant and specific to be a coincidence."

Mac toggled to the next few screens while explaining the evidence. "These undiscovered letters between members of the criminal organization within the Freemasons covering centuries of communications link this murder seated in front of you to the death of Mr. Lopezsanchez," Mac said, dramatically pointing to Thomas Balleck.

"After you listen to all of the facts of this case and take this evidence back with you into the jury deliberation room, you will be certain beyond any reasonable doubt that the financial ties among the Masonic lodges, these wealthy treasure hunters, and their shell companies, and this murder are part of an orchestrated case of smuggling illegal artifacts in our country. Thomas Balleck was engaged by fellow Masons to kill Mr. Lopezsanchez in order to cover up what would certainly be discovered. Deep-routed organized crime."

Mac took a seat. The courtroom remained silent.

Chapter 45

It wouldn't take long after all of the testimony and evidence was admitted for the jury to come back with a unanimous verdict of guilty on all counts as charged.

Rosemary Rodifer tried to argue in Balleck's defense that Mac's theories were nothing shy of some far-fetched conspiracy, but the evidence was overwhelmingly strong and solid.

Sentencing was a no-brainer, as Judge Redle knew that Balleck was already serving a life sentence.

This issue was how to handle to large media attention that this case caused, and how to protect the monuments in Wyoming and elsewhere from the new range of treasure hunters seeking to find their loot in a buried casque.

Protecting these casques would be complicated. But that was not Mac's job. Her job was to prosecute crimes, and she was good at it.

Chapter 46

The summer passed quickly for Mac and Burg, as they were outdoor enthusiasts and were most commonly spotted in the Bighorn Mountains enjoying Mother Nature.

One late afternoon while they were seated near their campfire after a successful day of fishing, Mac felt a strong ping on her left side. And then she felt another. She stood to get some relief and low and behold, her water broke. It was time to pack up quickly and get down the mountain and to the hospital. She was about to give birth.

Chapter 47

The twins were born later that evening. Luke and Matthew were strong and healthy and resting comfortably in Mac's arms. Burg couldn't stop crying. He had two sons.

Lucas Michael Burgess and Matthew Patrick Burgess were discharged with Mac and Burg the next day. They laid their babies in the middle of their King-sized bed and they both flanked them while lying on their sides, mesmerized by these two sleeping infants.

The doorbell had not stopped ringing and Burg was constantly interrupted by floral delivery and neighbors stopping by with casseroles and other goodies. They would not have to cook again for the rest of the year at this pace.

People stopped by to briefly get a look at the twins and to pay their respects to this couple. Mac, although a first-time mom, was a natural, and they settled in quickly to parenthood.

She did not want to take much time off for maternity leave, because crime didn't stop just because she gave birth. She did not want to return to the office to be overwhelmed by a backlog of cases.

Her paralegal was doing a great job sorting through everything and would prepare pleadings and deliver them to Mac's house for review and approval before filing them in court.

Mac would return to the office in due course, and she would not feel behind the eight ball for taking some time off as a new mother.

Burg took all of his paternity leave and then some. He had loads of vacation days saved up and he had competent deputies to handle the safety of the community. He wanted to savor every single second with his sons.

Burg had missed out on a lot of time when his daughters were born. He was new to the force in Cheyenne, Wyoming, and he didn't get paternity leave back in the day nor did he have saved up vacation time.

Now, he had both and intended to get full use of them so that Mac could go back to work and not feel guilty about being away from their babies.

It was working out well for their blossoming family.

Mac could not believe what a year she was having. It was like a dream come true.

www.ingramcontent.com/pod-product-compliance
Lightning Source LLC
Chambersburg PA
CBHW051242160726
47994CB00002B/991